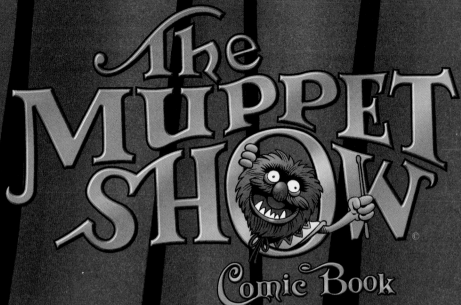

BOOM Kids!

ROSS RICHIE
chief executive officer

MARK WAID
editor-in-chief

ADAM FORTIER
vice president,
publishing

CHIP MOSHER
marketing director

MATT GAGNON
managing editor

JENNY CHRISTOPHER
sales director

FIRST EDITION: MARCH 2010

10 9 8 7 6 5 4 3 2 1

FOR INFORMATION REGARDING THE CPSIA ON THIS PRINTED MATERIAL
CALL: 203-595-3636 AND PROVIDE REFERENCE # EAST – 6593

On the Road

WRITER **Roger Langridge**

ART **Shelli Paroline & Roger Langridge**
PIGS IN SPACE · ON THE ROAD

COLORS **Digikore Studios, Mickey Clausen & Eric Cobain**

LETTERS **Shelli Paroline & Deron Bennett**
PIGS IN SPACE · ON THE ROAD

ASST. EDITOR **Jason Long**

EDITOR **Aaron Sparrow**

DESIGNER **Erika Terriquez**

COVER **Roger Langridge**

HARDCOVER CASE WRAP **Amy Mebberson**

SPECIAL THANKS: JESSE POST AND LAUREN KRESSEL OF DISNEY PUBLISHING, AND OUR FRIENDS AT THE MUPPETS STUDIO

"*TRUST* ME, FOZZIE...WHAT COULD POSSIBLY GO WRONG?"

WE COULD BE THROWN OUT, EMBARRASSED AND RIDICULED?

APART FROM THAT.

HEY, BABE! MR. *RAT* AND MR. *BEAR* TO SEE THE *BIG ENCHILADAS!*

I SEE... PLEASE TAKE A SEAT...

No PHOTOS (or artist renditions)

LOOKS KINDA *BUSY*...WE MIGHT BE WAITING A WHILE.

HEY--I'M A RAT! WATCH THIS.

⋛AHEM⋚ *GOSH, I SURE HOPE I REMEMBERED TO HAVE MY PLAGUE SHOTS!*

HEY, THAT'S CHEATING.

THANK YOU! SOMETIMES BEING A RODENT HAS ITS *ADVANTAGES.*

MISTER RAT AND MISTER BEAR? YOU'RE NEXT.

OKAY, REMEMBER-- *I* HANDLE THE BUSINESS STUFF! YOU JUMP IN WITH STORY DETAIL.

CHECK.

OKAY, YOU TWO-- THIS HAD BETTER BE *GOOD.*

OR AT LEAST FAST.

GOOD? WHY, IT'S *STUPENDOUS!* IT'S *COLOSSAL!* AND IT *AIN'T HALF BAD!*

IMAGINE, IF YOU WILL, *FLASH GORDON* MEETS *ANIMAL FARM...*

WAIT A MINUTE! HOLD IT RIGHT THERE!

AYYYYYUP?

AREN'T YOU A... YOU KNOW... A **RAT?** BECAUSE THIS PITCH ISN'T GOING ANY FURTHER UNTIL YOU **WASH YOUR HANDS!**

WASH MY...? ARE YOU GUYS **SERIOUS?**

SERIOUS AS **PLAGUE!** WE OVERHEARD THAT **CRACK** YOU MADE IN THE **WAITING ROOM!**

EVEN IF YOU **DON'T** HAVE PLAGUE, IT'S JUST GOOD HYGIENE.

OKAY, FOZZIE, OLD MAN... IT'S...IT'S UP TO **YOU** NOW! IF I DON'T COME BACK, TELL...TELL THE GALS BACK HOME I WAS THINKING OF THEM!

WILL DO, RIZZO. GOSH, I NEVER KNEW WASHING YOUR HANDS WAS SO **DANGEROUS.**

IT'S A VERMIN THING.

AAAHHH...WELL! YES! UH...OKAY. SO WE GOT THE PIGS, RIGHT? AND THEY'RE IN SPACE, OKAY?

IMAGINE NOW, IF YOU WILL, A PIECE OF NEWS THAT ROCKS THE EARTH TO THE VERY CORE!

AND NOW HERE IS A...

Sub-Etherwave **NewsFlash**

THIS JUST IN...

EVERYONE'S FAVORITE EVIL DICTATOR, *GONG THE GARRULOUS,* DENIES RUMORS THAT HE HAS HAD THE ENTIRE POPULATION OF GONGO *BRAINWASHED.*

SAYS GONG: "THEY DROOL BECAUSE OUR *FOOD* IS SO *DELICIOUS!"*

IN ENTERTAINMENT NEWS, *FLASH MCBUCK* HAS MARRIED THE FIVE-HEADED *PRINCESS HYDRA!* WHEN ASKED IF THIS WASN'T TECHNICALLY *BIGAMY,* HE REPLIED,

"IT'S POSITIVELY *ENORMOUS* OF ME. DO YOU HAVE ANY IDEA WHAT I SPEND ON EARRINGS?"

THE BELEAGUERED *CHICKEN PEOPLE OF B'GARK* GOT SOME GOOD NEWS TODAY WHEN IT WAS REVEALED THAT THEY WILL NO LONGER BE HARVESTED FOR THEIR FEATHERS.

THEY WILL INSTEAD BE HARVESTED FOR THEIR *DELICIOUS FLAVOR.*

ON THE *STOCK EXCHANGE,* MARTIAN CARBON IS DOWN TWO, THE COSMO IS UP NINE, SIX GETS A MISS, FIVE GETS TIME OFF FOR GOOD BEHAVIOR.

DON'T WORRY, I DIDN'T UNDERSTAND THAT EITHER.

AND FINALLY, IT HAS BEEN CONFIRMED THAT EARTH'S MOON HAS BEEN *WRENCHED* FROM ITS ORBIT BY *FORCES UNKNOWN!* THE *SWINETREK* HAS BEEN DISPATCHED TO RETRIEVE IT. A SPOKESMAN SAID, "WELL, THEY WERE EXPENDABLE."

THE MOON WAS UNAVAILABLE FOR COMMENT.

FIRE UP THIS **OLD CRATE**, GUYS -- WE HAVE TO GET MOVING PRONTO!

ON IT, LINK

YEAH -- WE ALREADY **KNOW** ABOUT THE **MISSION**.

MISSION? WHAT MISSION?

ER, TO FIND THE MOON? WHY **ELSE** DID YOU WANT TO LEAVE IN SUCH A HURRY?

PROMISE YOU WON'T TELL ANYONE...

I...I SAID SOMETHING **INAPPROPRIATE** TO THE **MARTIAN PRESIDENT'S DAUGHTER**. THE ENTIRE **MARTIAN DIPLOMATIC CORPS** IS AFTER ME!

GREAT! IF THIS **MISSION** DOESN'T KILL US, THE MARTIANS **WILL! PERFECTAMUNDO!**

HOLY MOLEY, LINK... WHAT DID YOU SAY TO HER TO PROVOKE SUCH AN **EXTREME REACTION?**

A-ALL I SAID WAS THAT TWO HEADS **SUITED** HER!

HOGTHROB...YOU MUST BE THE ONLY PERSON IN THE GALAXY WHO HADN'T HEARD ABOUT HER **UNSIGHTLY HEAD-SIZED MOLE.**

IT WASN'T **THAT** UNSIGHTLY.

KINDA **CUTE**, REALLY...

HI HO, **KERMIT THE FROG** HERE! TODAY WE'LL OBSERVE AN **ANCIENT KOOZEBANIAN RITUAL.**

I'LL USE THIS HANDY **TRANSLATOR** TO INTERPRET FOR YOU, LIVE! SHOULD BE EXCITING.

OKAY...THE FIRST GUY SAYS, "MAY THE SPIRIT OF MY ANCESTORS CONFER MANY BLESSINGS."

MIC MAK MOK MOK MOK!

OH DEAR. "YOUR **ANCESTORS?** YOU MEAN THAT **FREELOADING UNCLE** OF YOURS? THAT'S THE LAST TIME **HE** COMES FOR THANKSGIVING!"

HUBLURBLURB **ZING ZANG!**

MIC MAK MOK MOK MOK!

UH..."IT'S ALL **YOUR** FAULT FOR INVITING **AUNTIE PAT!** I **COULDN'T** LEAVE OFF UNCLE RALPH IF YOU INVITED AUNTIE PAT!"

"LISTEN, BUB, THE DAY I DON'T INVITE AUNTIE PAT IS THE DAY PIGS FLY!"

HURBLURBLURB ZING ZANG!

WHOOOOSH!

JOIN ME NEXT TIME WHEN WE'LL OBSERVE THE NOBLE KOOZEBANIAN ART OF **EEL-WRESTLING!**

UNTIL THEN... **WATCH THE SKIES!**

GOOD GRIEF. WHO'S THAT?

OH, THAT'S *S.T. WEETUMS* -- RIGHT-HAND MAN OF *GONG THE GARRULOUS.*

HE'S ONE OF OUR MOST *VALUED* CUSTOMERS!

KINDA. HE'S BEEN IN *MORE OFTEN,* EVER SINCE HE STARTED SCOUTING FOR *GONG'S COLLECTION...* OOPS!

I SEE... A *REGULAR,* IS HE?

SIGH... LOOK, I DON'T WANT YOU TO GET INTO TROUBLE. JUST TELL ME -- THIS COLLECTION -- DOES IT INVOLVE BIG SPHERES OF *LUNAR ROCK?*

WEEELLL...

MERCI.

OKAY, BOYS -- LET'S *MOVE!* WEETUMS' SHIP LEAVES IN FIVE AND WE'RE GOING TO *FOLLOW* IT!

B-BUT...BUT WE WERE *WINNING!*

DRAT YOU, PIGGY -- *DRAT YOU TO BITS!*

NOW, REMEMBER, BOYS -- HE MUSTN'T SEE US! IF HE DOES, WE CAN EXPECT TO BE TAKEN HOSTAGE AT BEST!

TRUST ME -- I WAS TOP OF THE *STEALTH MANEUVER CLASS* AT *SPACE CAMP!*

YOU WERE SAYING...?

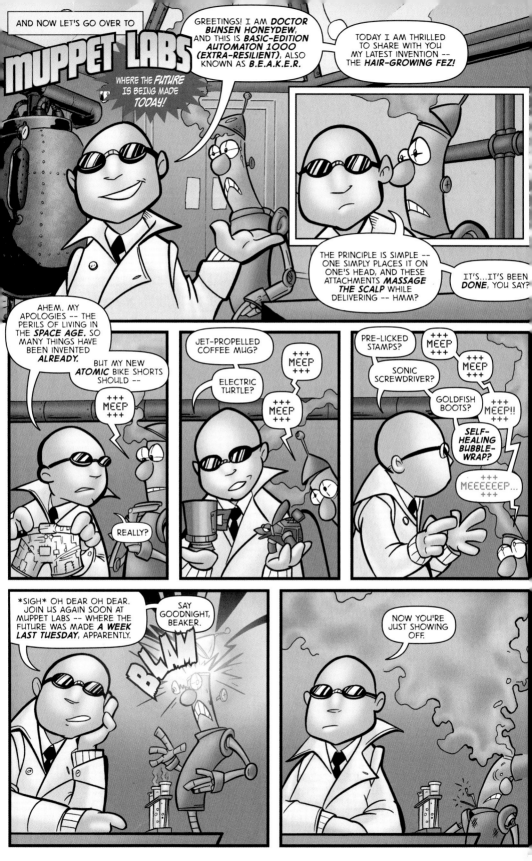

IT'S **STUPENDOUS**, I TELL YA! **EVERYBODY** LOVES CHICKENS!

RIZ-ZO!

I DUNNO, RAT. THE WHOLE BARNYARD FOWL THING IS **SO** 1987!

WE BELIEVE AUDIENCES WANT TO LEAVE THE THEATER WITH A **SMILE** ON THEIR FACES AND A SONG IN THEIR HEARTS...

...AND NO SWINE-COOKING CHICKENS WHATSO-EVER.

WAIT! Y-YOU HAVEN'T HEARD THE CLIMAX YET! TELL 'EM, FOZZIE!

YEAH! UH, WAIT, WHAT?

LOOKS LIKE I'M GONNA HAFTA DITCH THE WHOLE **INTERPLAN-ETARY POULTRY** NUMBER! THINK YOU CAN **BUSK** YOUR WAY TO AN **ALTERNATIVE ENDING?**

≥ULP!≤ I'LL DO MY BEST!

AH, WELL, YES! THE CLIMAX! YES! YES INDEED! AS WE WERE SAYING...

THIS HAD BETTER BE GOOD, BEAR.

AND FAST -- I'M DUE ON THE GOLF COURSE AT TWO.

TRUST ME -- THIS ONE WILL MAKE YOUR **BRAINS BURST** IN **THREE MINUTES FLAT!**

IMAGINE, IF YOU WILL, THE **DUNGEONS** BENEATH THE **ROYAL PALACE** OF **GONG THE GARRULOUS**...

WHAT A **STRANGE** MISUNDERSTANDING -- THE CHICKEN PEOPLE WERE MERELY GIVING US AN **HERBAL BATH!**

AND THAT GUY IN THE BASEBALL CAP WHO HANDED THEM THOSE **PINK PIECES OF PAPER** JUST BEFORE THEY DOUSED THE FIRE...WHAT WAS ALL **THAT** ABOUT?

WE'RE NOT OUT OF THE WOODS **YET**, BOYS...

CLANG

NOW WHAT?

WHY, NOW WE DO WHAT ANY SELF-RESPECTING PRISONER WOULD DO... WE TRY TO ESCAPE!

YEAH? DIG THROUGH STONE WALLS QUITE OFTEN, DO YOU?

BEHOLD -- MY **PEN-LASER!** WITH THIS LITTLE BABY, WE CAN BURN A TUNNEL OUT OF HERE IN AS LITTLE AS A **YEAR!**

HEY! NICE!

AMAZING AS IT SEEMS, BUBBLE-BRAIN, IT LOOKS LIKE YOU ACTUALLY GOT SOMETHING **RIGHT!**

MUCH, MUCH LATER!

BUK BUK BUK **BRRRRK!**

MOI?

BETTER GO QUIETLY, PIGGY...

WHZZZZZZZZZZZ

›ULP...‹ HELLOOOOO?

OKAY... I'M GOING TO TAKE A **BREAK** NOW. WHO'S NEXT?

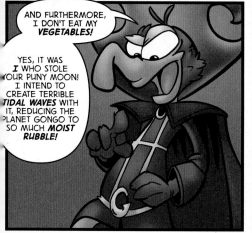

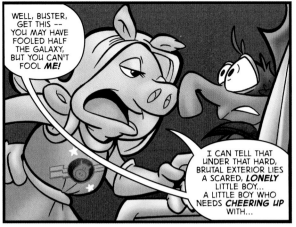

WELL, BUSTER, GET THIS -- YOU MAY HAVE FOOLED HALF THE GALAXY, BUT YOU CAN'T FOOL *ME!*

I CAN TELL THAT UNDER THAT HARD, BRUTAL EXTERIOR LIES A SCARED, *LONELY* LITTLE BOY... A LITTLE BOY WHO NEEDS *CHEERING UP* WITH...

...A SONG.

WHO'S THE GUY THE PEOPLE FEAR? DO YOU TREMBLE WHEN HE'S NEAR? SHOUT HIS NAME SO WE CAN HEAR -- *GONG THE GARRULOUS!*

SO TRUE!

WHO PUTS MOONS WHERE NONE BELONG? WHO IS ALWAYS IN THE WRONG? WHO NEEDS CHEERING WITH A SONG? *GONG THE GARRULOUS!* THAT'S WHO!

I SWEAR I'M JUST A CHEEKY SCAMP! A TIDAL WAVE JUST MAKES YOU DAMP!

BUK BURK BUK BUK BUK BUK BUK BUURRK?

GONG THE GARRULOUS! IT'S YOU!

RRRRMMMMBLLLLE

BUT WAIT! I HEAR A *SOUND*, YOU KNAVE!

IT'S GOT TO BE THAT *TIDAL WAVE!*

I WISH I FELT A WEE BIT *BRAVE...*

THE MOON WILL SEND YOU TO YOUR *GRAVES!*

THIS WHOLE SCENARIO'S ABSURD!

PERHAPS THE WORST I'VE EVER HEARD!

WHAT WE NEED IS A FRIENDLY WORD...

D-DOES THIS MEAN... FUNDING IS DEFERRED?

LET'S KEEP THE SEA FROM *COMING*, CREW!

WE'LL NEVER STOP IT -- *THINK IT THROUGH!*

BUT REALLY, WHAT *ELSE* CAN WE DO?

THIS IS THE *END*, I'M TELLING YOU!

WHAT'S THAT? AS IF WE NEEDED MORE!

IT'S COMING FROM THE *YONDER DOOR!*

RRRRRMMMMBLLLLLE

I-I THINK I KNOW! NOW, DON'T GET SORE... I LEFT THE FAUCET *ON* BEFORE!

YOU'VE DONE A *DUMB* AND *RECKLESS* THING!

OF *COURSE!* THAT'S PART OF BEING *KING!*

A *BRACE* IS WHAT THIS DOOR DEMANDS!

ALL THIS BECAUSE I WASHED MY --

OKAY, SO *PIGS IN SPACE* IS A NO-GO. FAIR ENOUGH. HOW ABOUT THIS...

"TALKING HOUSES -- THE NEXT GENERATION!"

YOU LIKE?

UH-OH.

WAYNE AND WANDA NIGHT FEVER?

GLOM

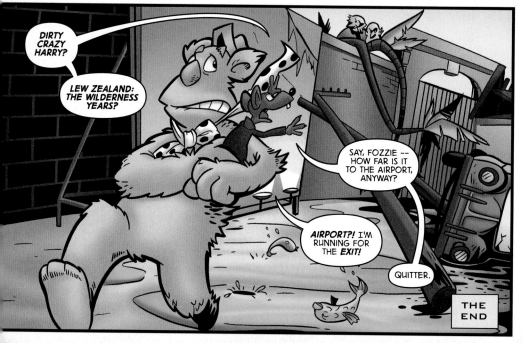

DIRTY CRAZY HARRY?

LEW ZEALAND: THE WILDERNESS YEARS?

SAY, FOZZIE -- HOW FAR IS IT TO THE AIRPORT, ANYWAY?

AIRPORT?! I'M RUNNING FOR THE *EXIT!*

QUITTER.

THE END

On the Road

HERE IS A...

THIS JUST IN:

KING KONG TODAY **DENIED** RUMORS THAT HE IS A FIFTY FOOT APE. ACCORDING TO HIS LAWYERS, HE IS **FIFTY-TWO FEET SIX INCHES.**

SCANDAL ERUPTED THIS AFTERNOON WHEN IT WAS REVEALED THAT MR. KONG HAD IN FACT BEEN **STANDING ON A CHAIR.** MR. KONG SAID, **"MWUUAAARGHH!".** CARPENTERS ARE INVESTIGATING.

IN **SPORTS NEWS,** THERE WERE RED FACES ALL AROUND TODAY DURING A COMPETITION TO SEE WHO HAD THE REDDEST FACE.

FINANCE! THE STOCK MARKET REMAINS BUOYANT IN ITS NEW HEADQUARTERS INSIDE A BLIMP. AMBULANCES ARE STANDING BY.

AND FINALLY, WHILE THEIR THEATER IS UNDERGOING REPAIRS, THE MUPPETS ARE TAKING THEIR SHOW ON THE ROAD! THEY'RE COMING TO A TOWN NEAR **YOU!**

ARE YOU GONNA **MOVE ON** OR DO I HAFTA **MAKE YA?** I'M WAITIN' TO LET THE **COWS** IN.

OKAY, SCOOTER--TURN LEFT UP AHEAD...

KERMIT-- I'M WORRIED ABOUT THIS WHOLE *ITINERANT PERFORMER* BUSINESS. I SEE THIS AS A MASSIVE STEP *BACKWARDS* FOR MY *CAREER!*

MAP

GEE, PIGGY, YOU *KNOW* WE CAN'T AFFORD TO CLOSE DOWN COMPLETELY.

BESIDES--IT'LL BE *FUN!* WE'RE GOING *BACK TO OUR ROOTS!*

ROOTS, SCHMOOTS. WITHOUT THE HIGH CLASS AMBIANCE OF THE THEATRE, OUR PERFORMANCES WILL SEEM *INCONGRUOUS*...EVEN *GAUCHE, N'EST-CE PAS?*

OH ME...OH MY. THIS WILL ALL END IN TEARS, I JUST *KNOW* IT.

ONION SANDWICH?

AAAND HERE WE ARE!

MISTER O'GRAVY? KERMIT THE FROG-- WE SPOKE ON THE PHONE.

CALL ME *"BAGS".* REMIND ME--WERE YOU WANTING THE *CARAVANS* OR THE *TIGER?*

ER, THE CARAVANS...?

GOOD, BECAUSE I CAN'T FIND THE TIGER. I FEEL LIKE SUCH A *FOOL!* TO LOSE *ONE* TIGER IS MERELY *UNFORTUNATE,* BUT TO LOSE *TWO* SEEMS LIKE *CARELESSNESS.*

HERE'S THE *MONEY* WE AGREED ON. DO YOU MIND IF I ASK WHY YOU'RE SELLING THE CARAVANS SO *CHEAPLY?*

⸙SIGH⸙ WELL, TO CUT A LONG STORY SHORT, I *LOST THE CIRCUS.* IT'S SO EMBARRASSING-- TO LOSE *ONE* CIRCUS IS MERELY *UNFORTUNATE...*

RIGHT, RIGHT.

ALL EXCEPT THE *TIGER,* OF COURSE. DO YOU HAVE ANY IDEA HOW *DIFFICULT* IT IS TO SELL A CARAVAN WHEN THERE MIGHT BE A *TIGER* LURKING IN ONE OF THE *WARDROBES?*

AAAHH. REALLY? AH.

OKAY, YOU ALL HEARD THAT-- BE *REALLY CAREFUL* WHEN YOU OPEN THE WARDROBES! ⸙GULP⸙

BETTER YET, *DON'T OPEN* 'EM.

KERMIT?

YES, FOZZIE?

I...I'VE DECIDED I WON'T COME AFTER ALL. I THINK I'LL STAY *HERE* A WHILE--DO SOME *STREET PERFORMING...* I THINK I NEED TO STAND ON MY OWN FOR ONCE.

WELL SURE, FOZZIE--I MEAN, IF THAT'S WHAT YOU NEED, I GUESS WE--

THANKS, FOZZIE...

GREAT! THANKS, KERMIT--I'LL MEET YOU GUYS BACK AT THE *MUPPET THEATER* IN A FEW MONTHS! GOOD LUCK WITH THE *TOUR!*

YOU'LL BE MISSED, MY FRIEND.

THE MUPPET ROADSHOW

featuring the EFFERVESCENT **MISS PIGGY**

THE EVER-KINETIC **GREAT GONZO**

THE ELFIN CHARM of **KERMIT THE FROG**

and MORE! MORE! MORE!

MUSIC! THRILLS! LAFFS!

ONE PERFORMANCE ONLY

HMM... MUPPET ROADSHOW?

HEY, YOU OLD FOOL! GET A LOAD OF THIS! THAT SHOW YOUR *COUSIN* WROTE TO YOU ABOUT IS PLAYING IN *OUR TOWN!*

HUH. YOU THINK WE SHOULD GO ALONG? WHAT IF IT'S AS BAD AS HE *SAYS* IT IS?

IMPOSSIBLE! I'VE GOT *GALLSTONES* THAT ARE BETTER THAN THAT!

AND SO...

PLEASE DONATE WHATEVER YOU THINK IS FAIR! MY *FRIENDLY ASSISTANT* WILL MOVE AMONG YOU WITH A *HAT.*

YOU THINK THAT'S *FAIR,* DO YUH?

W-WELL... I GUESS THE ORPHANAGE DOESN'T REALLY NEED *ALL* OF THIS...

ANY CHANCE OF GETTING THIS SHOW ON THE *ROAD?*

YEAH-- PREFERABLY *ROUTE 66!* HO HO HO!

CLICK

AND NOW, LADIES AND GENTLEMEN...

...THE MUPPET SHOW! YAAAYYYY!!

IT'S TIME TO PARK THE WAGONS! IT'S TIME TO PICK A SITE! IT'S TIME TO GET THINGS STARTED ON THE MUPPET SHOW TONIGHT!

IT'S TIME TO POST SOME POSTERS! IT'S TIME TO START A FIGHT-- IF YOU DON'T PAY SOME MONEY FOR THE MUPPET SHOW TONIGHT!

THE DÉCOR IS APPALLING... THE DANCING MAKES ME CURSE!

ACCORDING TO YOUR COUSIN, IT'S GONNA GET MUCH WORSE!

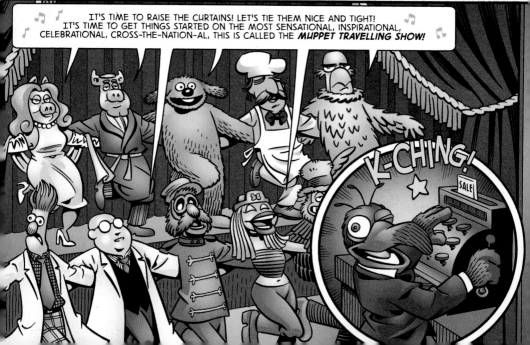

IT'S TIME TO RAISE THE CURTAINS! LET'S TIE THEM NICE AND TIGHT! IT'S TIME TO GET THINGS STARTED ON THE MOST SENSATIONAL, INSPIRATIONAL, CELEBRATIONAL, CROSS-THE-NATION-AL, THIS IS CALLED THE *MUPPET TRAVELLING SHOW!*

KL-CHING!

SALE

AND NOW IT'S TIME FOR... VETERINARIAN'S MEDICINAL COMPOUND
MOST EFFECTATIOUS IN EVERY CASE!

GOOD EVENING, LADIES AND GENTLEMEN! I AM THE FAMOUS DOCTOR BOB, WITH DEGREES FROM THE UNIVERSITIES OF ⇒MUMBLEMUMBLE⇐ AND ⇒HRRUMPH!⇐

I'M HERE TO TELL YOU ABOUT MY NEW, CURES-ALL-ILLS *MIRACLE POTION!* MAY I HAVE A *STRANGER* FROM THE *AUDIENCE?*

ME! OOH! *PICK ME!*

AH, TONY OLD PAL!

DOCTOR BOB!

I MEAN -- TONY, A PERSON I'VE *NEVER* MET BEFORE NOT EVEN EVER!

SLUURP!

DOCTOR BOB! *LOOK WHAT YOU'VE DONE TO THE PATIENT!*

GREAT! I WAS AFRAID WE'D HAVE TO CHANGE MY *BUSINESS CARDS* FOR A MINUTE THERE!

WAIT A MINUTE...

PLOP

WHY, DOC... I- I FEEL... LIKE A *MILLION DOLLARS!*

HEY, NURSE PIGGY--GET A *SHRINK!* THIS GUY THINKS HE'S A MILLION DOLLARS.

OH, BROTHER.

WILL DOCTOR BOB MAKE IT OUT OF TOWN? WILL LINK HOGTHROB BURST? WILL NURSE PIGGY EVER CATCH THAT EPISODE OF "DOCTOR HOG" SHE MISSED? DON'T MISS *LITTLE GIDEON, OHIO,* WHERE YOU'LL HEAR DOCTOR BOB SAY...

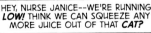

HEY, NURSE JANICE--WE'RE RUNNING *LOW!* THINK WE CAN SQUEEZE ANY MORE JUICE OUT OF THAT *CAT?*

ON IT, DOCTOR BOB!

IT'S THE *LOOK ON THEIR FACES* THAT KEEPS ME GOING.

NICE WORK, GUYS! *SAVE* ME A BOTTLE!

FER SHUUUURE!

OH, IT'S ALL WRONG! IT'S JUST ALL *WRONG!*

WHAT'S THE PROBLEM, PIGGY?

IT'S *THIS!* WITHOUT THE *THEATER,* EVERYTHING FEELS... *MANNERED! ARTIFICIAL!* NOT TO MENTION *DOWNRIGHT CHEESY!* MY *ADORING PUBLIC* DESERVES *BETTER!*

I KNOW, PIGGY, BUT WE NEED TO KEEP THE SHOW GOING SO THE CAST CAN GET *PAID!* I MEAN, I FUNDED THIS ROAD SHOW OUT OF MY OWN POCKET! IF YOU COULD JUST BE A LITTLE... *I DON'T KNOW,* FLEXIBLE...

NO, KERMIT -- MY MIND'S MADE UP! I'LL DO WHAT I MUST, BUT YOU CAN COUNT ME OUT OF THE *CLOSING NUMBER. I PREDICT A FIASCO!*

TOUGH COOKIE.

YOU SAID IT, MISTER WEAZELL.

BUT BACK TO BUSINESS. AS PER OUR *AGREEMENT,* IN EXCHANGE FOR YOU USING *MY LAND* FOR YOUR SHOW, I GET *HALF* YOUR TAKINGS.

UM...AFTER *EXPENSES,* SURELY?

NOPE. *FINE PRINT,* FLIPPER.

WELL, UH, CAN YOU *WAIT?* BECAUSE WE SPENT MOST OF IT ON *WAGES* ALREADY... IT WAS THE ONLY WAY TO GET THE CAST TO GO *ON...*

YOU'VE GOT UNTIL THE *END OF THE SHOW,* FROG. EITHER I WALK AWAY FROM HERE WITH *THREE HUNDRED DOLLARS* IN MY POCKET, OR I CALL THE *COPS!*

≶GULP≶

AND NOW...

★ ★ ★ ★ ★

A Message From

SAM THE EAGLE

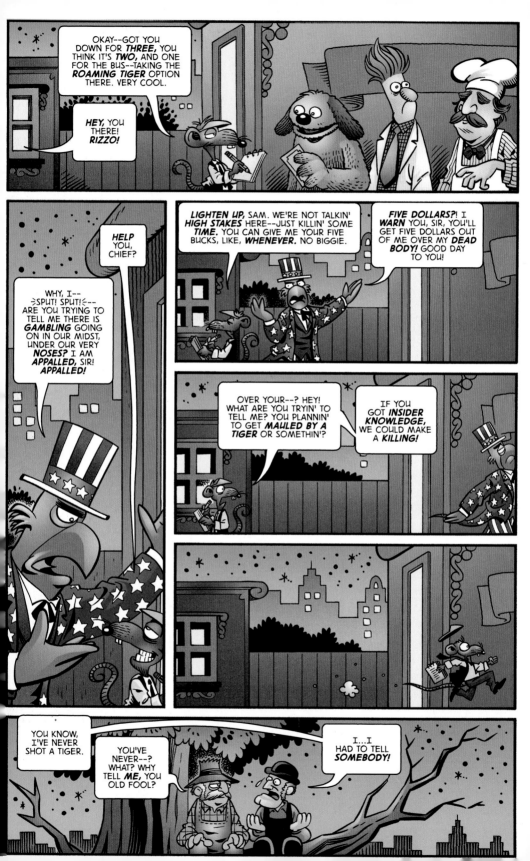

KERMIE! YOU **KNOW** THE THEATER ATMOSPHERE IS NECESSARY TO **FRAME** THE EXPERIENCE FOR THE **AUDIENCE!**

OUTDOOR THEATER WORKED FOR THE ANCIENT GREEKS AND SHAKESPEARE--IT'LL WORK FOR **US!**

HMMPH!

ANYHOW, IT'S TIME I CHECKED ON THE **CLOSING NUMBER.** THANKS TO YOU, GONZO'S HAD TO PUT SOMETHING TOGETHER AT **VERY** SHORT NOTICE...

GONZO! HOW'S IT GOING?

EASY, GIRLS... EEEAASSYYYY...

BUK BUK BUK BUK
BUK BGARK! BUK
BUK
FLOOMPH!

VERY NICE. ER, IS THAT **IT?**

HECK, NO! I DIDN'T EVEN GET A CHANCE TO JUGGLE THE **HAMSTERS**, NEVER MIND THE **FLAMING TOASTERS.** BUT EVERY TIME WE GET TO THAT POINT, THE GIRLS GO TO **PIECES...**

...BECAUSE THAT **WEASEL** KEEPS **STARING** AT THEM!

HEY--IS IT **MY** FAULT THEY'RE NERVOUS AROUND WEASELS?

THEY'RE **CHICKENS**, YOU'RE A **WEASEL!** THE CIRCLE OF LIFE CAN BE SCARY SOMETIMES.

LISTEN--I'M LOOKING FOR ONE OF MY PHEASANTS. I THOUGHT MAYBE IT WAS HIDING WITH YOUR WEIRD PAL'S **FEATHERED FRIENDS.**

LOOKS LIKE I WAS **WRONG**--I **HOPE.** FOR **YOUR** SAKE.

THREE HUNDRED DOLLARS, POND-BOY.

≶GULP≶

WHISPERING

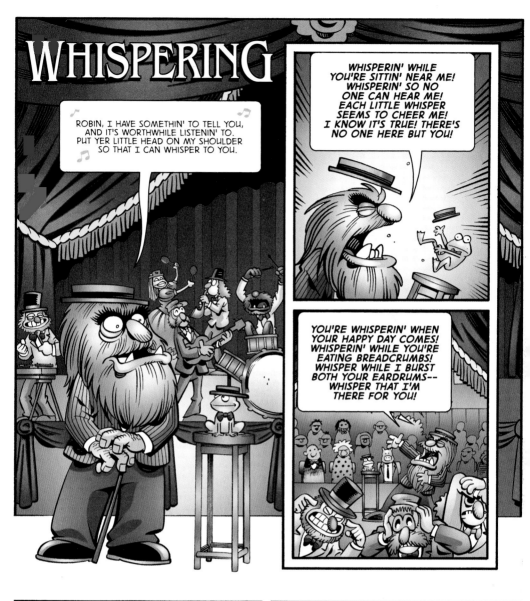

ROBIN, I HAVE SOMETHIN' TO TELL YOU, AND IT'S WORTHWHILE LISTENIN' TO. PUT YER LITTLE HEAD ON MY SHOULDER SO THAT I CAN WHISPER TO YOU.

WHISPERIN' WHILE YOU'RE SITTIN' NEAR ME! WHISPERIN' SO NO ONE CAN HEAR ME! EACH LITTLE WHISPER SEEMS TO CHEER ME! I KNOW IT'S TRUE! THERE'S NO ONE HERE BUT YOU!

YOU'RE WHISPERIN' WHEN YOUR HAPPY DAY COMES! WHISPERIN' WHILE YOU'RE EATING BREADCRUMBS! WHISPER WHILE I BURST BOTH YOUR EARDRUMS-- WHISPER THAT I'M THERE FOR YOU!

GOING DEAF IS A SIGN OF OLD AGE!

WHAT'S THAT?

I SAID, GOING DEAF IS A SIGN OF OLD AGE! HO HO HO!

NO MORE BETS, LADIES AND GENTLEMEN! I REPEAT, *ALL BETS ARE OFF!* WE HAVE A *WINNAH!*

≥GULP≤ WHAT'S UP, RIZZO?

WE, ER, *FOUND THE TIGER*, BOSS.

I'LL SAY! LOOK--I *CLEANED UP!*

WELL, UH, THAT'S GOOD, I--NO, *WAIT!* THAT'S *TERRIBLE!*

HONEST, KERMIT-- IT'S *OKAY!* I'VE HAD WORSE FROM FALLING OFF MY MOTORBIKE INTO A POOL OF *PIRANHAS.*

AND HE *MADE BANK*, LOOK! *THREE HUNDRED BUCKS!*

OKAY, YOU MADE A FEW DOLLARS, BUT YOU WERE, YOU KNOW, *MAULED BY A TIGER!* IS THAT REALLY *WORTH* IT?

WELL, ACTUALLY... YEAH. THIS IS *YOURS.*

HUH?

STRAIGHT UP--THE GANG PLACED A BET IN *YOUR NAME.*

WE KNOW YOU PAID FOR THE ROAD SHOW OUT OF YOUR *OWN POCKET*, KERMIT--TO KEEP THE SHOW GOING WITHOUT A *THEATER.* YOU DID THAT FOR US, AND WE WANTED TO SHOW YOU OUR APPRECIATION.

WE LOVE YOU, BUDDY.

GEE...I DON'T CARE ABOUT THE MONEY, OF COURSE...AND I'M NOT HAPPY ABOUT THE *TIGER* INCIDENT...BUT *THANK YOU.*

GOOD THING YOU DON'T CARE ABOUT THE *MONEY.*

PLEASURE DOING BUSINESS WITH YOU, MISTER FROG!

SLAM

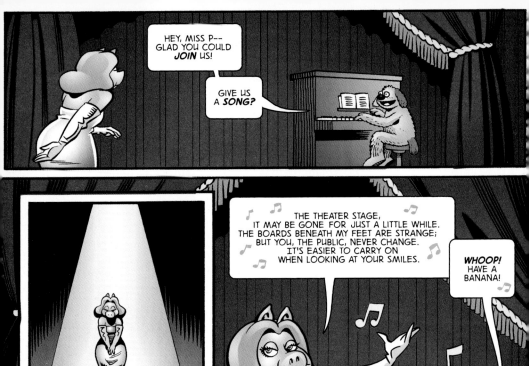

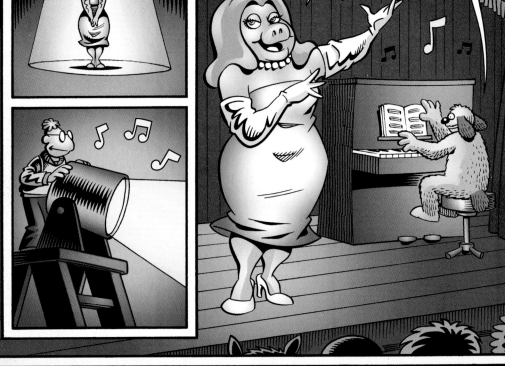

LATER...

BREAK IT TO US *GENTLY*, SCOOTER...WHAT'S OUR SITUATION?

WELL, AFTER *LAND RENTAL*, *WAGES*, GONZO'S *MEDICAL BILLS*, AND PAYING OFF THE LADY IN THE FRONT ROW WHO THREATENED TO *SUE* US FOR *MENTAL CRUELTY*...WE'RE LEFT WITH A GRAND TOTAL OF...

...THREE DOLLARS AND TWENTY-SEVEN CENTS.

OKAY! WELL, THERE IT IS. LOOK ON THE BRIGHT SIDE-- AT LEAST WE'RE IN THE *BLACK*, JUST. LET'S ALL GET SOME REST...WE'VE GOT A *LONG DAY* TOMORROW.

I DID LIKE YOU *SAID*, BOSS-- I AVOIDED USING THE WORD *"DISASTER"*.

THANKS. NO SENSE IN *DEMORALIZING* THEM...MAYBE THINGS WILL BE BETTER IN LITTLE STATWALD.

I'M KEEPING 'EM CROSSED.

OH, KERMIE? A *WORD*, IF I MAY...?

YOU DON'T HAVE TO SAY IT, PIGGY--I *KNOW*. YOU--

I CAN'T BELIEVE HOW *WRONG-HEADED* I WAS EARLIER. *CONGRATULATIONS!* THE MUPPET ROADSHOW IS AN *UNQUALIFIED SUCCESS!*

HUH?

WITH THE THEATRE OUT OF ACTION, IT WOULD HAVE BEEN SO *EASY* TO LET EVERYTHING FALL APART... BUT *YOU* KEPT IT ALL *TOGETHER!* YOU WERE *ABSOLUTELY RIGHT!* OH, KERMIE...CAN YOU *FORGIVE* SILLY, SILLY MOI?

WELL, I...UH...

OH, BLESS YOU, BLESS YOU. *MMMWAH!*

À BIENTÔT, KERMIE!

ER...MUD IN YOUR EYE.

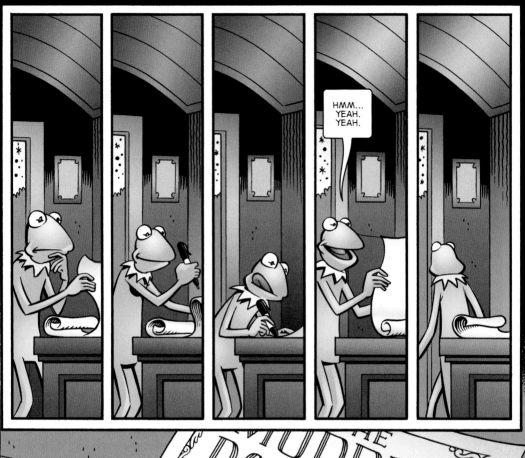

ALPHABEAR

Starring FOZZIE BEAR!

★ ★ ★

FOZZIE BEAR
WILL ENTERTAIN
? YOU ?
AT PRECISELY
3 PM
DONATIONS WELCOME

BEAR

CROWD

DROLLITY!

EXPECTATION	**F**AILURE	**G**ENTLEMEN!

HECKLERS!	**I**NSULTED	**J**OKES!

KIPPER	**L**AUGHTER	**M**ISERY

NIGHT!	**O**PTIMISM	**P**UNCHLINES

The End

...YEAH! YOU KNOW WHY? BECAUSE THERE'S NOT *MUSHROOM* INSIDE! GEDDIT?

SEE, IT WAS SUPPOSED TO BE A PLACE FOR *FUN GUYS* TO GO...*FUNGHIS*, GEDDIT?

IT'S ANOTHER WORD FOR MUSHROOM.

WHAT!? AM I TOO HIP FOR THE BUS STOP?

WAIT A MINUTE, HERE'S ONE. THREE GUYS WALK INTO A DOG KENNEL. AND THE *FIRST* GUY GOES, "WHAT ARE WE DOING IN A DOG KENNEL?" SO THE *SECOND* GUY GOES, "WELL..."

W-WAIT! LOOK--THE *BUS!* WE'RE SAVED! *SAVED!!*

OH, HALLELUJAH.

ABOUT TIME! IN ABOUT ANOTHER MINUTE, I WAS GOING TO BREAK MY *PAROLE.*

I'M A *COMEDIAN*...

...AND I'M GOING TO BE ON *THE MUPPET SHOW.*

CLINT WACKY

FILLING THE WORLD WITH LAUGHTER SINCE 1972

WAIT A MINUTE--YOU'RE NOT GETTING ON THIS BUS *TOO,* ARE YOU, MISTER--WHAT *IS* YOUR NAME, ANYWAY?

ME? OH, NO, NO. I'M WAITING FOR A RIDE. THE NAME'S *WACKY*, MA'AM. *CLINT WACKY.*

LET'S SEE... NEXT TOWN WE PLAY IS CALLED *LITTLE STATWALD.* SAYS HERE IT'S NAMED AFTER *TWO FAMILIES* WHO LIVE THERE.

ARE WE THERE YET?

ARE WE THERE YET?

ARE WE THERE YET?

MAP

APPARENTLY, EVERY RESIDENT IS *RELATED* TO ONE OF THE TWO FAMILIES.

SMALL TOWNS, DON'T YOU JUST LOVE 'EM?

ARE WE THERE YET?

ARE WE THERE YET?

WHUMMPP

HMM... GOOD SUSPENSION.

SHAME ABOUT THE *BRAKES...*

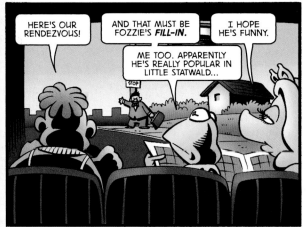

HERE'S OUR RENDEZVOUS!

AND THAT MUST BE FOZZIE'S *FILL-IN.*

I HOPE HE'S FUNNY.

ME TOO. APPARENTLY HE'S REALLY POPULAR IN LITTLE STATWALD...

STOP

CLINT WACKY, I PRESUME?

WACKY BY *NAME,* WACKY BY *NATURE. ESCHEW THE MUNDANE,* I SAY! *ESCHEW! ESCHEW!*

GESUNDHEIT. CLIMB ABOARD.

THANKS. DO YOU MIND *WAITING* A MINUTE? MY *SCRIPTWRITERS* ARE COMING WITH ME. THEY'LL BE HERE ANY MOMENT.

REALLY?

SCRIPTWRITERS? I THOUGHT *THIS* GUY WAS SUPPOSED TO BE THE TALENT.

SOME COMEDIANS JUST *WORK* THAT WAY, SCOOTER. AND I GUESS THERE'S ALWAYS ROOM FOR ONE MORE...

WACKY BY NAME, WACKY BY NATURE. *HYAK!*

THAT'S *TWO* MORE.

I AM MISTER *STADLER* AND THIS IS MISTER *WALTORF-- COMEDY WRITERS EXTRAORDINAIRE,* AT YOUR SERVICE!

STEP ON THE *GAS,* JUNIOR--WE CAN'T WAIT TO GET TO LITTLE STATWALD TO SEE THE *FOLKS* AGAIN!

UMM.

LITTLE STATWALD
10 miles

THE MUPPET ROADSHOW
featuring SPECIAL GUEST CLINT WACKY · FOR A LIMITED TIME!

...SO I THOUGHT WE'D START WITH ROBIN AND THE BOYS, GET EVERYBODY IN A *GOOD MOOD*, THEN PUT YOU ON *AFTER*.

DON'T WANT TO PEAK TOO *EARLY*, EH? FINE--IT'LL GIVE ME TIME TO REHEARSE MY *GENIUS!*

"THE MUSKRAT TOADSHOW"? WHAT'S THAT?

PUT YOUR *GLASSES* ON, YOU OLD FOOL! IT'S *"THE MULLET SNOWPLOUGH"!*

HEY, KERMIT--HAVE YOU *SEEN* THAT CROWD? THERE'S SOMETHING ODD ABOUT THEM...EVEN BY MY STANDARDS.

WHAT...? LET'S TAKE A PEEK...

HOLY SMOKES. THERE REALLY *ARE* ONLY TWO FAMILIES IN THIS TOWN, AREN'T THERE?

PART OF ME IS *GLAD* FOZZIE DECIDED TO STAY BEHIND AND DO *STREET THEATER* FOR A WHILE. HE WOULDN'T LIKE THIS AT *ALL.*

YEP...AND YET PART OF ME WISHES HE WERE HERE *RIGHT NOW.*

...ONLY A MATTER OF TIME BEFORE HOLLYWOOD COMES *KNOCKING*, OF COURSE...*HYAK!*

STILL, IN THE *PROUD TRADITION* OF THE MUPPET SHOW, LET'S MAKE THE BEST OF WHAT WE HAVE...

GONZO? GET THE BOYS. IT'S *SHOWTIME.*

LADIES AND GENTLEMEN, WELCOME TO *THE MUPPET SHOW*--WITH OUR VERY SPECIAL GUEST STAR, *CLINT WACKY!* YAAAYYYY!

AND NOW, WITHOUT FURTHER ADO, WE BRING YOU--*THE SONG OF THE WOODLAND GERBILS!*

VERY NICE, GUYS! UHH, KEEPS EVERYBODY ON THEIR TOES!

MISTER WACKY? YOU'RE UP NEXT!

I DON'T *HAVE* TO BE DOING THIS, YOU KNOW. I'VE WORKED WITH SOME OF THE FINEST *SINGING DENTISTS* THIS INDUSTRY HAS TO OFFER!

AND NOW, LADIES AND GENTLEMEN...THAT *MASTER OF MIRTH*... THAT *MAESTRO OF MERRIMENT*...CLINT WACKY!

HEY, DID YOU HEAR ABOUT THE GOLD NUGGET WHO *ROBBED A BANK?* IT WAS *GILTY!* GEDDIT? GEDDIT? ARE YOU GUYS AS *DEAF* AS YOU ARE *UGLY?*

... IS THAT YOUR *BEARD* OR DO YOU HAVE A SMALL *VOLE* ON YOUR CHIN?...

MAN! ALL THIS GUY DOES IS *ABUSE THE AUDIENCE!*

YEAH...BUT THEY SEEM TO BE *LAPPING IT UP.* MAYBE IT'S A *LITTLE STATWALD* THING.

HEH HEH HEH! "GEEE, LADY, YOU'RE UGLY!" *YOU'RE UGLY!!* I DON'T KNOW WHERE HE GETS THEM FROM!

HE GETS THEM FROM *US*, REMEMBER? OH, MISTER WALTORF-- HOW DROLL! HOW *VERY* DROLL! HO HO HO!

HA HA HA HA HA HA HA HA HA HA

KERMIT! LET *ME* WRITE SOME NEW STUFF FOR HIM. I'M NO FOZZIE, BUT THIS INSULT HUMOR IS INSULTING.

I HATE TO SAY IT... BUT THE GUY'S A *HIT!*

DO YOU WANT OUR SHOW TO BE REMEMBERED FOR TELLING THE AUDIENCE HOW UGLY THEY ARE?

...BLAH BLAH BLAH...

WELL, I...

ACTUALLY, NO. YOU'RE RIGHT. THERE ARE TIMES A LINE HAS TO BE DRAWN. DO WHAT YOU CAN, SCOOTER...

...JUST KILLING TIME HERE UNTIL *HOLLYWOOD* CALLS, REALLY...

...DO WHAT YOU CAN.

...AND THEN I TOLD BROADWAY, *"ABSOLUTELY NOT! I NEED SOMETHING THAT'S GONNA STRETCH MY RANGE! PORTRAYING A TEENAGE GIRL ISN'T CHALLENGING ENOUGH."*

I'VE BEEN PLAYING *HARD TO GET* EVER SINCE. OF COURSE, I'M REALLY WAITING FOR *SPIELBERG* OR *LUCAS.* IT'S ONLY A MATTER OF *TIME...*

MISTER WACKY! *MISTER WACKY!*

SQUIRTER, DEAR BOY! SOMETHING ON YOUR *MIND?*

THAT'S *SCOOTER,* AND YES-- I WAS WONDERING IF YOU'D MIND TAKING A LOOK AT SOME *MATERIAL* I WROTE. I'M SURE ONCE YOU *READ* IT YOU'LL SEE HOW --

AH-AH-*AH,* SNOOTER. LET'S NOT PRE-EMPT THE *ACT OF DISCOVERY.*

WHEEET

WH-- WHAT? WHAT ARE YOU--

AHA! *UNAUTHORIZED MATERIAL!*

IN DIRECT *CONTRAVENTION* OF CLAUSE 4, PARAGRAPH 3(A)IIII!

BUT THEN...THAT'S HARDLY *LIKELY,* IS IT? WHY WOULD YOU TAMPER WITH *GENIUS?*

I THINK YOU'LL FIND THAT I'M ENTITLED TO *EXTREME* COMPENSATION IF I'M (A) *FIRED* OR (B) HAVE MY MATERIAL *ALTERED* IN ANY WAY!

CONTRACT

THERE THEY GO... AND WITH THE *ONLY COPY* OF MY SCRIPT!

HEY, SCOOTER...ALL IS NOT LOST. THERE ARE *OTHER* THINGS YOU CAN TRY.

THINGS? *WHAT* THINGS?

RIZZO SAYS HE CAN MAKE CLINT *QUIT* OF HIS *OWN ACCORD.*

CAN I *EVER.*

TIME PASSES!

DON'T MIND US! JUST SETTING UP FOR THE NEXT ACT.

CLACK CLACK CLACKETY CLACK CLACK

"...AND AS FAR AS THIS REVIEWER IS CONCERNED, WACKY COULDN'T BE LESS FUNNY IF HE WAS A DISEASE!" HMM...HARSH.

CLACK CLACK CLACK CLACKETY CLACK

YEAH--APPARENTLY KERMIT'S GOT *AMPHIBIAN LURGI. HIGHLY* CONTAGIOUS!

YOU DON'T SAY. IS THAT THE ONE WHERE THAT *ENTIRE VILLAGE*--

I KNOW. *TRAGIC,* ISN'T IT?

CREW   CREW   CREW

CLACK CLACKETY CLACK CLACK CLACK

...AND, UH, AS A *BIG* FAN OF YOURS, I'D LIKE T' GIVE YUH A GREAT BIG *KISS.*

IN YER OWN TIME, O' COURSE. NO *PRESSURE* OR NOTHIN'.

CLACK CLACK CLACK CLACKETY CLACK

I WONDER IF THEY'RE TRYING TO TELL ME SOME-THING.

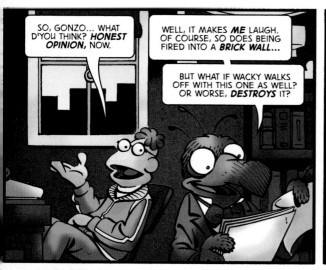

SO, GONZO... WHAT D'YOU THINK? **HONEST OPINION**, NOW.

WELL, IT MAKES **ME** LAUGH. OF COURSE, SO DOES BEING FIRED INTO A **BRICK WALL**...

BUT WHAT IF WACKY WALKS OFF WITH THIS ONE AS WELL? OR WORSE, **DESTROYS** IT?

DON'T WORRY-- I'M KEEPING **CARBON COPIES** OF EVERYTHING NOW. I'M NOT LOSING ANY MORE OF MY **HARD WORK**.

WELL, ALL I CAN SAY IS, **BE CAREFUL.** TRY TO MAKE HIM THINK IT'S **HIS** IDEA OR SOMETHING.

...I DON'T THINK YOU APPRECIATE MY SITUATION, SCHOONER! WHY WOULD I WANT **YOUR** SCRIPT? FRANKLY, I'M JUST **KILLING TIME** HERE UNTIL **HOLLYWOOD** CALLS!

B-BUT... BUT...

THE IDEA THAT I'D SPEND TIME MEMORIZING **NEW MATERIAL!** REALLY!

"AFTER ALL...THE GUY'S GOT QUITE AN **EGO**."

HEY, MISTER WACKY--WE'VE GOT THOSE **NEW PAGES** WRITTEN!

YES--WE LIFTED THE JOKES FROM SOME **VERY EXPENSIVE** CHRISTMAS CRACKERS!

WA HEY **HEY!**

SEEYA, KID.

SLAMM

LATER...

♪

CLINT WACKY

TELEGRAM FOR **MISTER WACKY!**

AAH, SLIDE IT UNDER THE **DOOR**, WILLYA?

NO CAN DO, CHIEF! **PERSONAL DELIVERY ONLY!**

CLINT WA

UNLESS YOU WANT ME TO SEND IT STRAIGHT BACK TA **HOLLYWOOD...?**

HOLLYWOOD?! LET ME SEE THAT!

...MUTTER MUTTER... "...TAKE GREAT PLEASURE IN OFFERING YOU THE **LEADING ROLE** OPPOSITE **LOLA VAVOOM** IN VINCE TACKLE'S NEW COMEDY BLOCKBUSTER, **'NO TIME FOR TABOULI.'"** HOT DOGGIES!

≥COUGH COUGH≤ AHEM AHEM **AHEM!**

ONE SIDE, LOSERS! OUT OF MY WAY-- **SHOO,** I SAY! **SHOO! SHOO!**

GESUNDHEIT.

WHAT WAS ALL **THAT** ABOUT?

LOOKS LIKE OUR WACKY FRIEND FINALLY GOT THAT **CALL FROM HOLLYWOOD** HE'S BEEN TELLING US ABOUT. HE'S **GONE--AT LAST!**

GONE?

B-BUT...BUT **HE'S** THE **CLOSING NUMBER!** NOW WE'VE GOT A **HUGE HOLE** IN THE SHOW...AND WE'VE GOT **FIVE MINUTES** TO **FILL IT!**

OOPS.

WHERE ON EARTH ARE WE GOING TO FIND SOMEBODY WITH A **PREPARED ROUTINE** OF **FUNNY MATERIAL** AT SUCH SHORT NOTICE?

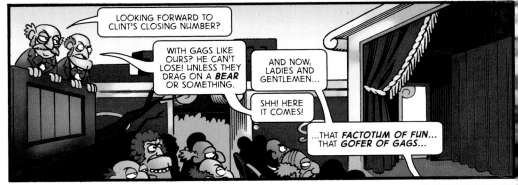

LOOKING FORWARD TO CLINT'S CLOSING NUMBER?

WITH GAGS LIKE OURS? HE CAN'T LOSE! UNLESS THEY DRAG ON A *BEAR* OR SOMETHING.

AND NOW, LADIES AND GENTLEMEN...

SHH! HERE IT COMES!

...THAT *FACTOTUM OF FUN*... THAT *GOFER OF GAGS*...

...*SCOOTER!*

HUH??

HOWDY HOWDY HOWDY, FOLKS! SAY, DID YOU HEAR ABOUT THE *TURKEY* WHO CROSSED THE ROAD? IT HAD A DATE WITH A *CHICKEN!*

B-DUM TSS!

BOOO! LAME!

TOO SOON! *TOO SOON!*

TERRIBLE! YOUR CHRISTMAS CRACKERS MUST BE *INCREDIBLY* CHEAP!

YEAH! THEY'RE PROBABLY NOT EVEN *THIS YEAR'S!*

AH...THEN THERE'S THE ONE ABOUT THE *DONKEY* WHO STUDIED *TECTONIC PLATES*...

HEY, KID-- YOU GOTTA *DITCH THE SCRIPT!* IF YOU DON'T TAKE *CONTROL* OF THIS CROWD, THEY'LL *EAT YOU ALIVE!*

WHAT-- YOU MEAN *IMPROVISE?*

DON'T WORRY-- *ANIMAL* WILL BACK YOU UP!

B-DUM TSS!

WHAT'S THE HOLD-UP? *GET OFF!*

MAYBE HE'S WAITING FOR *CONTINENTAL DRIFT!* HO HO HO!

⋝GULP!⋜

LOOK AT HIM-- HE'S JUST STANDING THERE!

THIS MUST BE SOME NEW COMEDY TECHNIQUE-- MAKE THE *SCENERY* LOOK FUNNY BY *COMPARISON!* HO HO HO!

I-I'M SORRY, SIR, I COULDN'T MAKE OUT WHAT YOU SAID. I TH-THINK YOUR MOUTH MIGHT BE FULL OF *GARBAGE.*

B-DUM TSS!

HA HA HA HA HA HA HA HA HA HA HA HA HA HA

BOOO! THIS IS THE WORST SHOW I'VE EVER SEEN!

AND THAT'S *SAYING* SOMETHING--HE'S GOT A SEASON TICKET TO *VINCE TERRIBLE'S ALL-CHIMPANZEE AMATEUR DRAMATIC SOCIETY!*

REALLY? PERHAPS YOU SHOULD LET *THEM* WRITE YOUR MATERIAL NEXT TIME! I HEAR THOSE BOYS CAN WORK *WONDERS* WITH AN INFINITE NUMBER OF TYPEWRITERS!

B-DUM TSS!

HA HA HA HA HA HA HA HA HA HA HA HA

HA HA HA HA HA HA HA HA

OKAY.

I USED TO KNOW A SINGING PONY WHO HAD TO *QUIT* BECAUSE HE WAS A *LITTLE HORSE*...

HA HA HA HA HA HA HA HA HA HA HA HA HA HA HA HA HA HA HA HA HA HA HA HA

CORNFLAKES ARE TRICKY, AREN'T THEY? I CAN NEVER GET ALL THE *PIECES* TO *FIT TOGETHER*...

HA HA HA HA HA HA HA HA HA HA HA HA

SCOOTER DID GREAT!

ANOTHER DISASTER AVERTED!

BUT I'M CURIOUS ABOUT WHAT MADE CLINT WACKY *TEAR OFF* IN SUCH A HURRY.

GOOD RIDDANCE!

OH, WELL...THE MAIN THING IS, THE SHOW WENT ON. I GUESS THAT'S *ALWAYS* THE MAIN THING.

LATER, GUYS.

AU REVOIR, KERMIE.

WOW. IS THAT SCOOTER'S *TRASH?* HE REALLY *SWEATED* OVER THAT MATERIAL!

SCOOTER

GOFER
NERAL ADMIN
ETC.

"YOU'D LIKE MY PAL FOZZIE--THE *THREE BEARS* WERE HIS *FOREBEARS*..."

HEH! EVEN THE *REJECTED* STUFF ISN'T HALF BAD!

WHAT'S *THIS?*

..."VINCE TACKLE'S NEW COMEDY BLOCKBUSTER, *'NO TIME FOR TABOULI.'* PLEASE RESPOND TO PINE NUT STUDIOS *WITHOUT DELAY.*"

TELEGRAM

WELL, IT WASN'T THE NICEST THING TO DO, BUT... I CAN'T SAY I *BLAME* HIM. YOUR SECRET IS SAFE WITH *ME*, SCOOTER.

THAT GUY IS *FULL* OF SURPRISES.

WHICH JUST GOES TO SHOW...YOU CAN SOLVE THE MOST INTRACTABLE PROBLEMS WITH *WORDS.*

WITH A MIND LIKE THAT, THAT KID'LL *GO* PLACES. AND I WISH HE'D LEAVE NOW....HEHEHEH! I STILL GOT IT!

The End

PAAACKAGGGE FOORRR *FOOOZZZZZIIIE BEEEARRR?*

GIVE IT TO ME, SON-- I'LL SEE HE GETS IT. HE AIN'T HERE RIGHT NOW, BUT WE'RE EXPECTIN' HIM FOR THE *BIG OPENING.*

KIIINDA *BIIIG.*

YEAH?

SPEEECIAAALLLL FFFRRRIIIGHT.

SPECIAL FRIGHT? DON'TCHA MEAN SPECIAL *FREIGHT?*

AAAUGHH!!

NNNNNNOOOOOOOO.

And now... **THE GONZO MARATHON**

Stage One

HELLO, AND WELCOME. THIS IS *LOUIS KAZAGGER*, AND TODAY WE'LL BE JOINING *GONNN-ZO THE GRRRREAT* AS HE COMMENCES HIS CHARITY FUND-RAISING *COMBINATION PERFORMANCE ART* AND *MARATHON*.

RIGHT NOW HE'S GETTING READY TO START, SO WITHOUT FURTHER ADO LET'S TALK TO THE...*UH, WHATEVER HIMSELF.*

SO, GONNN-ZO, TELL ME AND THE READERS--WHAT'S IT ALL *ABOUT?*

WELL, LOUIS, IT SEEMED TO ME LIKE THE PERFECT OPPORTUNITY TO DO SOMETHING *ARTISTIC* WITH THE TIRED OLD *MARATHON FORMAT.* I'LL BE TRAVELLING IN A VARIETY OF *UNUSUAL* WAYS THROUGHOUT THE RUN.

VERRR-RY INTERESTING. AND TELL US--WHAT'S WITH THE *WETSUIT?*

CANALS, LOUIS, *CANALS!* MY GOAL IS TO DO THIS IN A *STRAIGHT LINE!* NONE OF THIS WIMPY *GOING AROUND* THINGS! DO I LOOK *CHICKEN* TO YOU?

B- GURRRRR...

SORRY, CAMILLA.

BANG FLOP FLOP FLOP

ANNND THERE HE GOES! WITHOUT DOUBT THE STRANGEST THING I'VE SEEN SINCE BREAKFAST. EGGS WITH MAPLE SYRUP! WHAT WEIRDO CAME UP WITH THAT?

WE'LL UPDATE THROUGHOUT THE RUN, BUT FOR NOW--*BACK TO THE STUDIO!*

BEAUREGARD, YOU'RE A **TREASURE!** WHY, THIS PLACE IS LOOKING AS **GOOD AS NEW!**

GEE, **THANKS,** MISS PIGGY. A LITTLE MORE **DUST** ON THE FLOOR AND A FEW MORE **COBWEBS** AND I'LL BE ABOUT **DONE.**

EXIT

PUSH

KERMIT...I MUST ASK YOU... WILL WE, AT LONG LAST, BE PERFORMING **CHECKHOV?**

THAT'S A VERY GOOD QUESTION, SAM. **NO.**

FINE. JUST CHECKING.

HEY, KERMIT...SEEN THIS? IT'S ADDRESSED TO **FOZZIE.**

I DUNNO. **LUGGAGE?**

KINDA...**NO-FRILLS** FOR LUGGAGE.

LET'S DEAL WITH IT **LATER,** SCOOTER. WE'VE GOT A SHOW TO DO!

OKAY--LET'S GET THIS SHOW ON THE **ROAD...**ER, I MEAN **OFF** THE ROAD AND INTO A **THEATER! PLACES, EVERYBODY!**

IT'S TIME TO PLAY THE MUSIC...IT'S TIME TO LIGHT THE LIGHTS...

LOOK AT THAT! NO SENSE OF RHYTHM. AND THAT **SINGING!**

SINGING? I THOUGHT SOMEBODY WAS **STRANGLING A CAT!**

WAIT A MINUTE, WE USED THE CAT LINE **LAST YEAR.**

HMMPH. "SITTING ON BAGPIPES?"

BETTER. BETTER.

1001 TOP HECKLES

NEXT:

MUPPET LABS

MUPPET LABS

WHERE THE FUTURE IS BEING MADE TODAY!

GREETINGS! I AM DOCTOR BUNSEN HONEYDEW, AND THIS IS MY QUIVERING YET LOYAL ASSISTANT, BEAKER.

MEEP.

AS YOU SAY, TODAY WE ARE GOING TO ATTEMPT A PRACTICAL DEMONSTRATION OF THE FAMOUS THOUGHT EXPERIMENT, SCHRODINGER'S CAT!

SIMPLY EXPRESSED, THE EXPERIMENT SUGGESTS THAT, ACCORDING TO QUANTUM THEORY, A THING MAY EXIST IN TWO DISTINCT STATES SIMULTANEOUSLY UNTIL EXAMINED BY AN OUTSIDE OBSERVER.

SCHRODINGER'S EXAMPLE USED A CAT. WE, ON THE OTHER HAND, WILL GO ONE BETTER.

GET DOWN, BEAKER! THIS WON'T HURT A BIT.

MEEEEEP! MEE MEE MEEP!

EARLIER, I PLACED TWO NECKTIES IN THE BOX--ONE RED, ONE GREEN. BEAKER WILL NOW PUT ONE TIE ON, IN THE DARK.

ACCORDING TO SCHRODINGER, THERE SHOULD NOW BE TWO BEAKERS IN THE BOX, ONE IN A RED TIE AND ONE IN A GREEN TIE. WE WON'T KNOW WHICH UNTIL WE OPEN THE BOX AND DETERMINE A SINGLE POSSIBILITY.

HERE YOU GO, POPS. THIS ONE HERE, IT WAS IN THE BOTTOM OF MY *SATCHEL* FOR A WEEK...

GOSHAROOTIE! LOOK WHO IT'S *FROM!*

HEY, EVERYBODY! *LOOKY HERE!* WE GOT A *LETTER* FROM *FOZZIE BEAR!*

FOZZIE! HE HASN'T FORGOTTEN US!

HAS THE FUZZBALL DECIDED TO ACTUALLY *SHOW UP FOR WORK* AT LAST?

HEY, MAYBE HE *LIKES* LIVING IN GARBAGE CANS. BELIEVE ME, I *SYMPATHIZE.*

"DEAR GANG...

"...my street performing is going well. I seem to be extremely popular with the constabulary.

"I feel the experience has sharpened my comic sKills. Earning enough daily to be able to eat a wide variety of exotic fruit and vegetables!

"UNFORTUNATELY, MY EXTRAVAGANT DINING HAS LEFT ME SHORT OF A BUS FARE HOME, BUT I THINK I'VE FIGURED OUT A WAY TO DO IT ON THE CHEAP. SEE YOU SOON! LOVE, FOZZIE."

GREAT-- SO HE'S *COMING?*

BY SOME *MYSTERIOUS MEANS,* APPARENTLY.

I WANT TO HEAR THE ONE ABOUT THE *DOG WITH NO NOSE* AGAIN. THAT'S, LIKE, MY *FAVORITE.*

SPEAKING OF MYSTERIOUS MEANS...I WONDER HOW *GONZO'S* GETTING ALONG?

THE GONZO MARATHON — STAGE TWO

WELCOME BACK TO THE *GONZO MARATHON.* LOUIS KAZAGGER WITH YOU ONCE AGAIN, TRACKING THE PROGRESS OF *THE GRRREAT GONNN-ZO* AS HE RAISES MONEY FOR *CHARITY.*

SO TELL ME, GONNN-ZO... WHAT'S WITH THE *TUB?*

WELL, LOUIS, I'M GLAD YOU ASKED. THIS IS MY ANSWER TO THOSE PEOPLE WHO RAISE MONEY FOR CHARITY BY SITTING IN A *BATHTUB FULL OF BEANS.* I FIGURE, WHY NOT COVER SOME *DISTANCE* WHILE I'M SITTING?

MMM. BUT WHY *OATMEAL?*

I LIKE OATMEAL!

WELL, FULL MARKS FOR AVOIDING THE OLD *BEANS* TRAP, ANYWAY. THIS ONE SEEMS *IMPOSSIBLE* TO TOP!

YOU'LL HAVE TO EXCUSE ME, LOU--IT'S TIME FOR MY *TROMBONE SOLO.* MY PUBLIC AWAITS!

I STAND CORRECTED.

WELL, AS YOU CAN SEE, *GREAT THINGS* ARE AFOOT. AND INDEED, *GREAT FEET* ARE A *THING!* WHAT WILL THE NEXT STAGE OF THE GRRREAT GONNN-ZO'S MARATHON CONSIST OF? ALL WE KNOW FOR CERTAIN IS, HE *WON'T STARVE.* NOW, BACK TO THE STUDIO!

PRRP PRRP MP PRRP PRRP

BOO! *BOOO!* CALL YOURSELF A *COMEDIAN?*

UM...ACTUALLY, I DON'T THINK HE *DOES.*

OH.

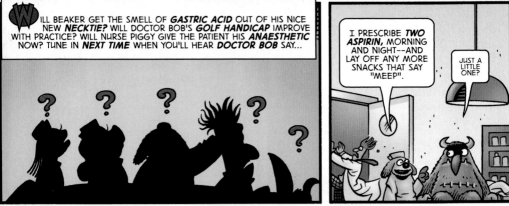

...AND IT SEEMS TO *ME*, KERMIE, THAT WE *OWE* IT TO FOZZIE TO *OPEN THE BOX.* SUPPOSE IT CONTAINS SOMETHING *PERISHABLE?*

YEAH! YEAH! SOMETHING *PERISHABLE!* LIKE *MONEY!*

SMAAAAASH BOX.

ALL RIGHT, *KNOCK IT OFF!*

I *KNOW* YOU'RE ALL CURIOUS, AND I *UNDERSTAND* THAT. I *REALLY DO.* BUT IT'S *NOT OURS.* IT *BELONGS TO FOZZIE.*

WE'LL PUT IT IN THE *BASEMENT,* WHERE WE WON'T HAVE TO *THINK* ABOUT IT ALL THE TIME. OKAY?

BOX WALK *AWAAAY!*

I TRUST YOU INTEND TO TAKE *FULL RESPONSIBILITY* FOR THE CONSEQUENCES OF YOUR DECISION, SIR.

KERMIT...YOU WON'T EVEN MAKE AN EXCEPTION FOR *MOI?*

SORRY, PIGGY...*MOVE ON,* GUYS. NOTHING TO SEE HERE.

HEY, FELLAS...DOES IT FEEL LIKE EVERYTHING'S *TIGHTLY PACKED* IN THERE, OR IS IT ALL SORT OF *ROLLING AROUND?*

UH, JUST A SORTA *DEAD WEIGHT* IN THE *MIDDLE,* I GUESS. HOW COME?

OOOHH, NOTHING... JUST...WONDERING.

OH.

LET'S FACE IT, WE'VE *ALL* WANTED TO OPEN IT. I DOUBT WE'RE GOING TO GET A *LICK OF WORK* DONE UNTIL THIS IS NO LONGER *ON OUR MINDS.* SO LET'S TAKE A VOTE: ALL THOSE IN *FAVOR...?*

AYE!!

THE AYES *HAVE* IT!

SORRY, FOZZIE...BUT THIS IS FOR THE *GOOD OF THE SHOW.*

SPUNG

FOZZIE!!

≥YAWN≤ AM I HERE *ALREADY?*

W-WHAT?--WHY?--HOLD IT, HOLD IT. YOU WERE IN THERE *ALL ALONG?*

OH YES! I WAS SHORT OF *CASH*-- BUT MADE ENOUGH IN *TIPS* TO *MAIL MYSELF HOME.*

A *BRILLIANT* PLAN!

AH, BUT WITH A *FATAL FLAW!* I ADDRESSED THE PACKAGE TO *MYSELF*--SO I HAD TO WAIT FOR SOME- BODY TO *OPEN IT!*

AS *ALWAYS,* FOZZIE, YOUR TIMING IS *IMPECCABLE.* CARE TO JOIN US FOR THE *CLOSING NUMBER?*

NOTHING KEEPING ME IN *THERE*...I WAS DOWN TO MY *LAST SANDWICH!*

HE'S NOT EVEN *FUNNY,* HE'S ONLY A *BEAR!*

HIS JOKES YOU DON'T *LAUGH* AT, YOU JUST *SIT* AND *STARE!*

HE KEEPS ON RETURNING-- BUT *WE* DON'T CARE! BECAUSE *FRUIT* IS GOOD FOR YOUR *HEALTH!*

THE AUDIENCE FREQUENTLY WON'T WANT TO KNOW! THEY LIKE TO SELECT A *PROJECTILE* TO THROW! SO I *HIT* IT AND SPRAY IT *ACROSS THE FRONT ROW!*

HE'S THE *BEAR* WHO *SHARES THE WEALTH!*

BUT THERE'S SOMEBODY *MISSING.* NOW WHO COULD IT BE? THERE'S A *GAP* IN THE CHORUS-- FOR *ONCE,* IT'S *NOT ME!* AND DO I HEAR A SOUND LIKE A *FARAWAY BEE...?*

SMASH

AAAAAAHHH!!

THUD

OOOOFF!!

I'M SORRY, GUYS--SO MUCH FOR STEALTH.

HEY! *WELCOME BACK,* FOZZIE!

...SO YOU TRAVELLED BY *LAND, SEA* AND *AIR*, IS THAT WHAT YOU'RE SAYING?

YEAH-- AND I THINK THE *CANNON* COUNTS AS *FIRE*.

AND ALL FOR *CHARITY!*

THAT WAS A VERY GENEROUS THING TO DO, GONZO. SO WHO'S THE LUCKY *BENEFICIARY?*

WELL, IT WAS GOING TO BE FOR THE *CHESSINGTON WASP SANCTUARY*, BUT THEY HAD A BIG *SCANDAL*. IT TURNS OUT SOME OF THE WASPS WERE JUST *MOTHS* PAINTED WITH *YELLOW STRIPES*.

OOOH, THOSE *MOTHS!* THEY ALWAYS HAVE TO *SPOIL EVERYTHING!*

SO I'M OPEN TO *SUGGESTIONS*.

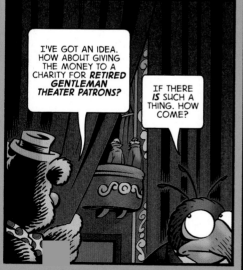

I'VE GOT AN IDEA. HOW ABOUT GIVING THE MONEY TO A CHARITY FOR *RETIRED GENTLEMAN THEATER PATRONS?*

IF THERE *IS* SUCH A THING. HOW COME?

SO...WHAT DID YOU *THINK?*

WASN'T IT, THOUGH?

ATROCIOUS. ABSOLUTELY *ROTTEN*.

IN FACT, I CAN'T REMEMBER THE LAST TIME I HATED *ANYTHING* THAT MUCH. I'M GOING TO TELL *ALL MY FRIENDS*.

THEY'RE DOING A *MATINEE* TOMORROW. LET'S COME ALONG AND *HATE THAT TOO!*

YOU'VE GOT YOURSELF A *DEAL*.

"OH, I DUNNO...I JUST THINK THEY *DESERVE* IT. DON'T YOU?"

EATER

The End

Cover Gallery

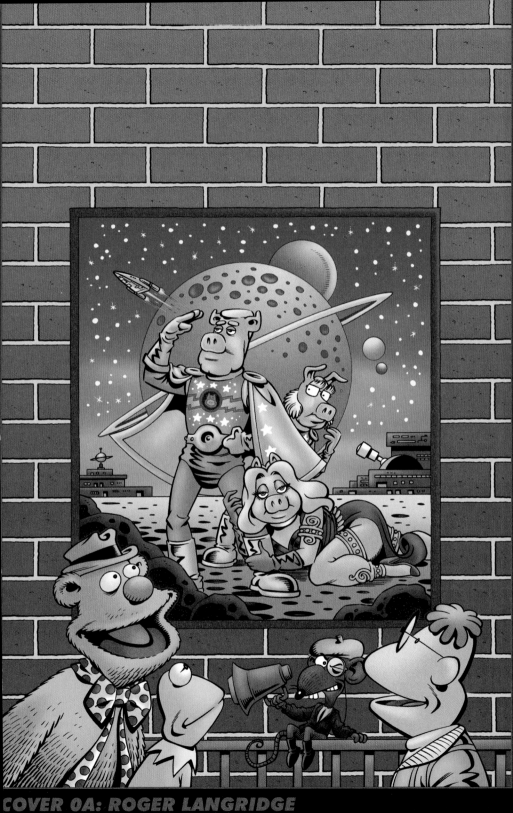

COVER 0A: ROGER LANGRIDGE

COVER 0B: ROGER LANGRIDGE

COVER OC: AMY MEBBERSON

COVER 1A: ROGER LANGRIDGE
COLORS / DIGIKORE STUDIOS

COVER 1B: ROGER LANGRIDGE
COLORS / DIGIKORE STUDIOS

COVER 1C: AMY MEBBERSON

ALSO: THE COMEDY STYLINGS OF **FOZZIE BEAR**

COVER 2B: ROGER LANGRIDGE
COLORS / ERIC COBAIN

ISSUE 2 EMERALD CITY COMIC-CON EXCLUSIVE:
AMY MEBBERSON

COVER 3A: ROGER LANGRIDGE

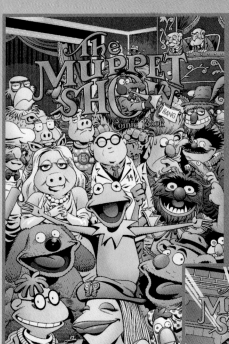

WALL-E: RECHARGE

Wall-E is not yet the hardworking robot we know and love. Instead, he lets the few remaining other robots take care of most of the trash compacting while he collects interesting junk. But when the other robots start breaking down, Wall-E must learn to adjust his priorities... or else Earth is doomed!

WALL E: RECHARGE
SC $9.99 ISBN 9781608865123
HC $24.99 ISBN 9781608865543

MUPPET ROBIN HOOD

The Muppets tell the Robin Hood legend for laughs, and it's the reader who will be merry! Robin Hood (Kermit the Frog) joins with the Merry Men, Sherwood Forest's infamous gang of misfit outlaws, to take on the stuffy Sheriff of Muppetham (Sam the Eagle)!

MUPPET PETER PAN

When Peter Pan (Kermit) whisks Wendy (Janice) and her brothers to the magical realm of Neveswamp, the adventure begins! With Captain Hook (Gonzo) out for revenge for the loss of his hand, Wendy and her brothers may find themselves in a situation where even the magic of Piggytink (Miss Piggy) can't save them!

MUPPET ROBIN HOOD
SC $9.99 ISBN 9781934506790
HC $24.99 ISBN 9781608865260

MUPPET PETER PAN
SC $9.99 ISBN 9781608865079
HC $24.99 ISBN 9781608865314

FINDING NEMO: REEF RESCUE

Nemo, Dory and Marlin have become local heroes, and are recruited to embark on an all-new adventure in this exciting collection! Their reef is mysteriously dying and no one knows why!

MONSTERS, INC.: LAUGH FACTORY

Someone is stealing comedy props from the other employees, making it difficult for them to harvest the laughter they need to power Monstropolis... and all evidence points to Sulley's best friend Mike Wazowski!

FINDING NEMO: REEF RESCUE
SC $9.99 ISBN 9781934506882
HC $24.99 ISBN 9781608865246

MONSTERS, INC.: LAUGH FACTORY
SC $9.99 ISBN 9781608865086
HC $24.99 ISBN 9781608865338

DISNEY'S HERO SQUAD: ULTRAHEROES

It's the year 2734 and the only one standing in the way of earth's utter destruction is...Mickey Mouse?! Join the four-colored fun as Mickey Mouse, Goofy, Donald Duck take to the skies to save the world.

DISNEY'S HERO SQUAD: ULTRAHEROES
SC $9.99 ISBN 9781608865437
HC $24.99 ISBN 9781608865529

WIZARDS OF MICKEY: MOUSE MAGIC

Your favorite Disney characters star in this magical fantasy epic! Student of the great wizard Grandalf, Mickey Mouse hails from the humble village of Miceland. Allying himself with Donald Duck (who has a pet dragon named Fafnir) and team mate Goofy, Mickey quests to find a magical crown that will give him mastery over all spells!

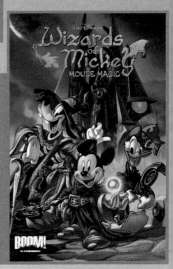

WIZARDS OF MICKEY: MOUSE MAGIC
SC $9.99 ISBN 9781608865413
HC $24.99 ISBN 9781608865505

DONALD DUCK AND FRIENDS: DOUBLE DUCK

Donald Duck as a secret agent? Villainous fiends beware as the world of super sleuthing and espionage will never be the same! This is Donald Duck like you've never seen him!

DONALD DUCK AND FRIENDS: DOUBLE DUCK
SC $9.99 ISBN 9781608865451
HC $24.99 ISBN 9781608865512

UNCLE SCROOGE: THE HUNT FOR OLD NUMBER ONE

Join Donald Duck's favorite penny pinching Uncle Scrooge as he, along with Donald himself and Huey, Dewey and Louie embark on a globe spanning trek to recover treasure and save Scrooge's "number one dime" from the treacherous grasp of Magica De Spell.

UNCLE SCROOGE: THE HUNT FOR THE OLD NUMBER ONE
SC $9.99 ISBN 9781608865536
HC $24.99 ISBN 9781608865536

THE LIFE AND TIMES OF SCROOGE MCDUCK VOL. 1
BOOM Kids! proudly collects the first half of THE LIFE AND TIMES OF SCROOGE MCDUCK in a gorgeous hardcover collection -- featuring smyth sewn binding, a gold-on-gold foil-stamped case wrap, and a bookmark ribbon! These stories, written and drawn by legendary cartoonist Don Rosa, chronicle Scrooge McDuck's fascinating life. See how Scrooge earned his 'Number One Dime' and began to build his fortune!

THE LIFE AND TIMES OF SCROOGE MCDUCK VOL. 2
BOOM! Kids proudly presents volume two of THE LIFE AND TIMES OF SCROOGE MCDUCK in a gorgeous hardcover collection in a beautiful, deluxe package featuring smyth sewn binding and a foil-stamped case wrap! These stories, written and drawn by legendary cartoonist Don Rosa, chronicle Scrooge McDuck's fascinating life.

THE LIFE & TIMES OF SCROOGE MCDUCK VOLUME 1 HC
HC $24.99 ISBN 9781608865383

THE LIFE & TIMES OF SCROOGE MCDUCK VOLUME 2 HC
HC $24.99 ISBN 9781608865420

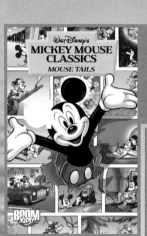

MICKEY MOUSE CLASSICS VOL. 1
See Mickey Mouse as he was meant to be seen! Solving mysteries, fighting off pirates, and just generally saving the day! These classic stories comprise a "Greatest Hits" series for the mouse, including a story produced by seminal Disney creator Carl Barks!

DONALD DUCK CLASSICS: QUACK UP
Whether it's finding gold, journeying in the Klondike, or fighting ghosts Donald will always have help with Huey, Dewey, Louie, his much more prepared nephews, by his side! Carl Barks brought Donald to prominence, and it's only fair to start off the series with some of his most influential stories!

MICKEY MOUSE CLASSICS: MOUSE MAYHEM
HC $24.99 ISBN 9781608865444

DONALD DUCK CLASSICS: QUACK UP HC
HC $24.99 ISBN 9781608865406

WALT DISNEY'S VALENTINE'S CLASSICS
Love is in the air for Mickey Mouse, Donald Duck and the rest of the gang. But will Cupid's arrows cause happiness or heartache? Find out in this collection of classic stories featuring all your most beloved characters from the magical world of Walt Disney! Featuring work by Carl Barks , Floyd Gottfredson, Daan Jippes, Romano Scarpa and Al Taliaferro.

WALT DISNEY'S CHRISTMAS CLASSICS
BOOM! Kids has raided the Disney publishing archives and searched every nook and cranny to find the best and the greatest stories from Disney's vast comic book publishing history for this "best of" compilation.

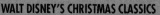

WALT DISNEY'S VALENTINES CLASSICS VOL 1 HC
HC $24.99 ISBN 9781608865499

WALT DISNEY'S CHRISTMAS CLASSICS VOL 1 HC
HC $24.99 ISBN 9781608865482